6/11

Finding Lincoln

Ann Malaspina   Paintings by Colin Bootman

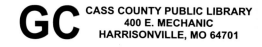
Albert Whitman & Company, Chicago, Illinois

Library of Congress Cataloging-in-Publication Data

Malaspina, Ann, 1957-
Finding Lincoln / by Ann Malaspina ; illustrated by Colin Bootman.
p. cm.
Summary: In segregated 1950s Alabama, Louis cannot use the public library to research a class assignment, but
one of the librarians lets him in after hours and helps him find the book that he needs. Includes an author's note
with historical information about library segregation in the South.
Includes bibliographical references.
ISBN 978-0-8075-2435-0
[1. Segregation—Fiction. 2. African Americans—Fiction. 3. Libraries—Fiction.
4. Lincoln, Abraham, 1809-1865—Fiction. 5. Alabama—History—1951—Fiction.]
I. Bootman, Colin, ill. II. Title.
PZ7.M28955Fi 2009 [E]—dc22 2008055551

The design is by Carol Gildar.

For more information about Albert Whitman & Company,
please visit our web site at www.albertwhitman.com.

For the brave children who walked into a segregated library and asked
to borrow a book.—A.M.

I dedicate this book to the inspiration and hard work of all librarians.
I would also like to thank Brandon Hines for his contribution in
making these illustrations possible.—C.B.

On his way home from school, Louis walked past the main library. The doors swung open, and Louis could see an enormous room filled with books. Why, there must be a million books in there, maybe more. Louis wished he could go inside and count them for himself.

PUBLIC LIBRARY
SINCE 1929

PUBLIC LIBRARY
SINCE 1929

The books reminded Louis that he had to write an essay on President Lincoln. But the library was for white people only, just like the strawberry milkshakes at the drugstore lunch counter, the swings in the city park, and the best seats at the movie theater.

It was 1951 in Alabama, and Louis could play all his piano scales and roller-skate backwards. Still he couldn't borrow a book from the main library.

"How about some lemonade?" asked Mama when Louis got home.

"I'm not thirsty." He sat down, kicking his foot against the table leg.

"What's the matter?"

Louis didn't feel like talking. He was thinking that Daddy always had books piled high by his bed. But he had read those books again and again. Now Daddy wanted a book on honeybees so he could learn how to keep beehives. If Mama was ever going to have fresh honey, Daddy needed to get inside that library, too.

"Maybe a little homework will cheer you up," teased Mama, as she let the biscuit dough rise for supper.

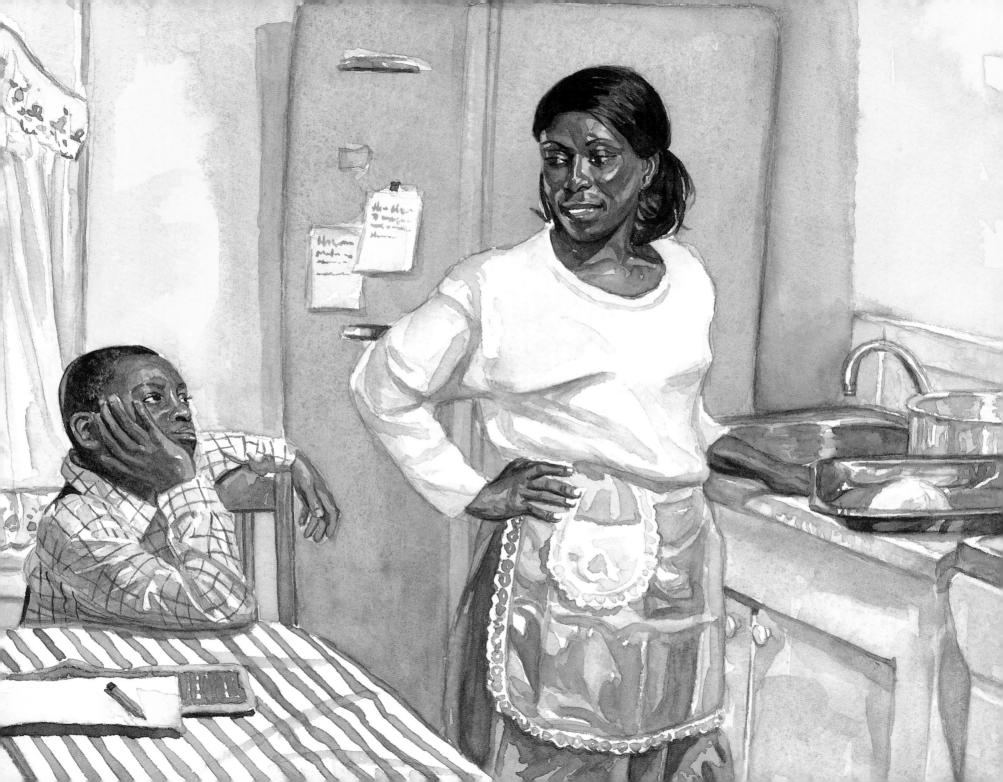

That morning, Mrs. Yates had told Louis's class about the Civil War. The North and the South went to battle over many things, including slavery. The Southern farmers said they needed slaves to plant the tobacco and pick the cotton. President Lincoln wanted the slaves to be free.

"He dared to stand up for what he believed in, and that made a lot of people mad," said Mrs. Yates.

Louis raised his hand. "Did President Lincoln shake things up when he was a boy?"

Mrs. Yates didn't know the answer. "Why don't you find out and write us an essay," she said, giving him a book about Lincoln.

But the book didn't say anything about *young* Abe.

Now Louis stared at his blank paper. "I need to find a book about President Lincoln when he was a boy," he told Mama.

"I have an idea," Mama said.

After the biscuits were baked, she took Louis to the basement of their church. She and her friends had started a small library where people donated books they didn't want anymore. Louis saw cookbooks, mysteries, and a book of maps, but no books about President Lincoln or honeybees.

"One day soon we'll be checking books out of the main library. Just you wait," Mama said on the way back home.

Louis didn't want to wait anymore.
And he wasn't going to!

The next day after school, Louis stopped in front of the main library. Holding his breath, he climbed the wide steps and pushed open the door. Everywhere he looked, books were shelved high. Louis didn't have time to count, but a million seemed about right. The library was also full of people. Every one of them turned to stare at Louis.

In the quiet room, Louis's heart was beating as loud as a tin drum. He began walking to the front desk. He was so nervous that he bumped into a man's chair.

"Watch where you're going, boy," said the man.

"Excuse me," mumbled Louis. On the polished floor, his sneakers squeaked like an old rusty hinge.

Two librarians sat at the desk, looking at him. "Can't you read?" said one, pointing at the "Whites Only" sign next to the door.

Louis's face burned like it did when he ran fast on a hot day in August.

The second librarian put down the book she was holding. "You'd better go home," she said, leading Louis back to the door.

As she gently pushed him outside, she whispered, "Come back tomorrow after five."

Louis didn't see how tomorrow would be any different. Still, Mrs. Yates was waiting for that essay. He had to go back.

The next afternoon, Louis told Mama he needed to run an errand. Before she could ask a question, he was off.

He ran all the way to the library and up the front steps. It was after five o'clock. The door wouldn't budge when he pushed it. Just as Louis turned to go, he heard a voice.

"Shh, come in quickly." The door cracked open, and the librarian from yesterday peeked out.

Inside, the library was dark and quiet.
"Now, what book did you want?" she asked.

"I need a book about President Lincoln
when he was a boy."

"Follow me."

Louis followed her down one stack of books,
then another. She stopped, moving her finger
along a high shelf.

"Here it is."

She pulled down a book. Her hand
was shaking, like Louis's insides. She
could get in big trouble for helping
him. She might have to pay a fine
or even lose her job.

Louis read the cover, *Abe Lincoln Grows Up,*
by Carl Sandburg. She had found just the
right book!

Then Louis thought of something. "Don't I need a library card?"

Even Daddy and Mama couldn't get a library card. Staring down at his sneakers, Louis wished he could disappear.

The librarian was quiet for a moment. Then she tapped him on the shoulder.

"Come on. I'll give you a temporary one. You do live in town, don't you?"

Louis raised his head. "Yes, ma'am." This librarian didn't seem to mind shaking things up at all!

Walking slowly down the street, Louis looked at the book and his library card all the way home.

Louis burst in the kitchen door. He couldn't wait to tell everybody.

When she heard what had happened, Mama threw up her hands in amazement.

Daddy shook his head like he had when Louis caught the catfish up at the lake last summer. "Isn't that something!" he kept saying.

Mama put her arm around Louis. "I hope no one got in trouble."

Daddy cleared his throat. "Mama and I just want you to be careful."

That night, Louis and Daddy read about young Abe and his kindness to animals. Though he grew up in the wilderness, Abe didn't like to shoot game. When he saw his friends hurting a turtle, Abe refused to join in. He didn't care if he wasn't like the other boys.

Abe also liked to have fun. Once he lifted a boy upside down so he could walk across the ceiling. Abe had to clean up the muddy footprints.

Abe could swing an ax, drive a plow, and win a wrestling match with anyone he met. What he liked best was to read a book. Some people said he was lazy and thought too much. Abe was just in a hurry to learn everything he could.

When Louis sat down to write his essay, he filled up three whole pages.

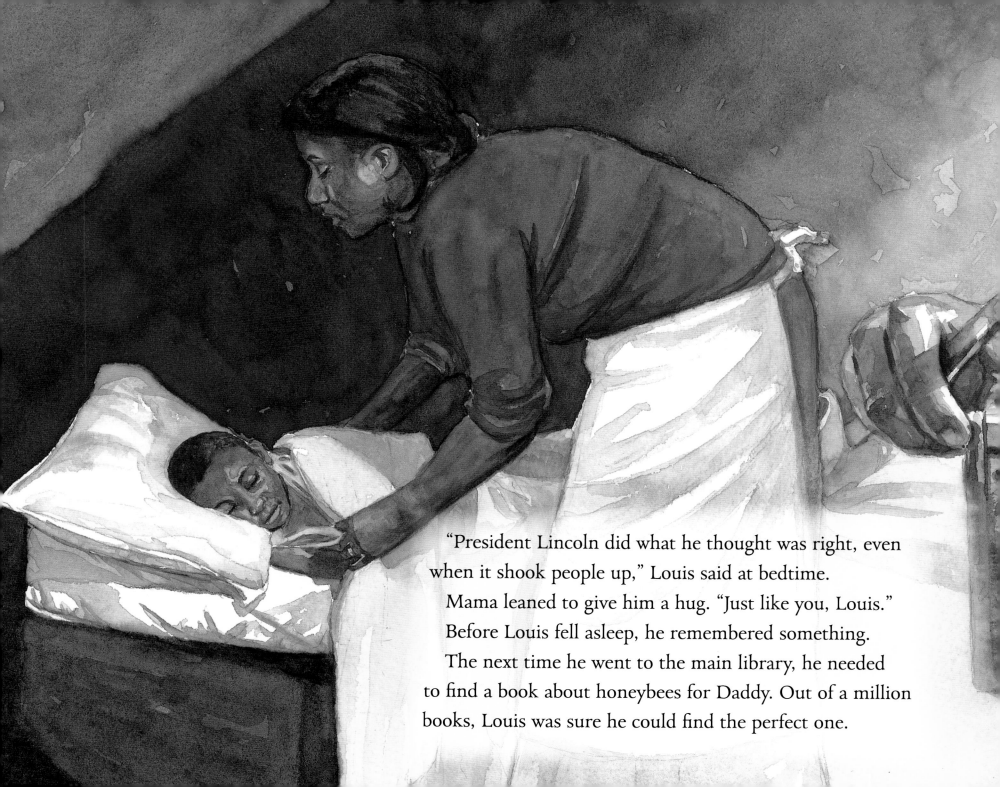

"President Lincoln did what he thought was right, even when it shook people up," Louis said at bedtime.

Mama leaned to give him a hug. "Just like you, Louis."

Before Louis fell asleep, he remembered something.

The next time he went to the main library, he needed to find a book about honeybees for Daddy. Out of a million books, Louis was sure he could find the perfect one.

NOTE

Like public schools, swimming pools, and drinking fountains, most libraries across the South, and in some states outside the South, were segregated until the 1960s. African Americans could not sit and read at the tables, or check out books. In 1950, a young boy in Troy, Alabama, wanted to take out a book from his local library. He knew he couldn't get a library card, but he and his brothers and sisters and cousins walked into the library anyway. The librarian told the children that the library was for whites only and not for "coloreds," remembers John Lewis, who went on to become a leader in the civil rights movement and a United States congressman from Georgia.

In segregated communities, the public library systems were supposed to provide "separate, but equal" services to African Americans. Many cities, such as Louisville, Kentucky, and Houston, Texas, opened branch libraries in churches, high schools, and other buildings. Sometimes bookmobiles brought library books into African American neighborhoods. African Americans got special library cards, stamped with "Negro" or "Colored." But the bookmobiles and branch libraries had smaller budgets, fewer books, and shorter hours. In fact, they were not at all equal to the main libraries.

During the 1960s, civil rights activists held nonviolent protests at segregated libraries. Even when libraries began to integrate, protests often followed. In Anniston, Alabama, a riot broke out and two African American ministers were injured when the public library was integrated in 1963. The next year, five African American men entered the whites-only library in Clinton, Louisiana. They were supposed to use the bookmobile instead. One of them, named Henry Brown, asked for a book called *The Story of the Negro*. The assistant librarian said she could order it, and he could pick it up at the bookmobile. But the men quietly sat down in protest of segregation at the library. The police arrested them for disturbing the peace and refusing to leave a public building, and the five men were tried and found guilty. The case reached the United States Supreme Court, which ruled in favor of the protestors in 1966. Justice Abe Fortas wrote in his majority opinion for *Brown v. Louisiana:* "Regulation of libraries and other public facilities must be reasonable and nondiscriminatory and may not be used as a pretext for punishing those who exercise their constitutional rights."

By the end of the 1960s, the Supreme Court and the federal government had put an end to laws allowing racial segregation. Libraries across the country finally opened their doors to everyone. And in 1998, Congressman Lewis was given an honorary library card at Alabama's Pike County Public Library.

PRESIDENT LINCOLN

Abraham Lincoln was born in a log cabin in Kentucky on February 12, 1809. Growing up in the wilderness, Lincoln spent little time in school, but he loved to read. "He wanted to learn, to know, to live, to reach out. . . . And some of what he wanted to know so much, so deep down, seemed to be in the books," wrote the American poet Carl Sandburg in his biography *Abe Lincoln Grows Up* (1928). Lincoln went on to become a lawyer and United States congressman from Illinois. In November 1860, he was elected the sixteenth president of the United States.

The next spring, the Civil War broke out between the South and the North. Lincoln was determined to unite the country. He also hated slavery and wanted to stop it from spreading. He took the first step to end slavery when he signed the Emancipation Proclamation on January 1, 1863. The slaves in states still fighting Lincoln's Union Army were now "forever free." But Lincoln wanted to do more. "If slavery is not wrong, then nothing is wrong," said Lincoln. He pushed Congress to abolish slavery in all states. Sadly, he did not live to see this happen. On April 14, 1865, as the Civil War was ending, Lincoln was shot. He died the next day. The Thirteenth Amendment to the Constitution became law on December 6, 1865. Slavery was finally abolished.

If You Want to Read More

Bradby, Marie. *More Than Anything Else.* New York: Scholastic, 1995.

Coleman, Evelyn. *White Socks Only.* Morton Grove, Illinois: Albert Whitman, 1999.

Coles, Robert. *The Story of Ruby Bridges.* New York: Scholastic paperback, 2004.

Miller, William. *Richard Wright and the Library Card.* New York: Lee and Low, 1999.

St. George, Judith. *Stand Tall, Abe Lincoln.* New York: Philomel, 2008.

Sandburg, Carl. *Abe Lincoln Grows Up.* New York: Harcourt Brace, 1928; paperback reissue,
   New York: Houghton Mifflin Harcourt, 2009.

Turck, Mary C. *The Civil Rights Movement for Kids. A History with 21 Activities.* Chicago: Chicago Review Press, 2000.

Weatherford, Carole Boston. *Freedom on the Menu: The Greensboro Sit-ins.* New York: Puffin, 2007.